James Frederick Mason, Stella Alys Wittram

Cupid's game wth hearts

A tale of Bloody Antietam

James Frederick Mason, Stella Alys Wittram

Cupid's game wth hearts
A tale of Bloody Antietam

ISBN/EAN: 9783337137366

Printed in Europe, USA, Canada, Australia, Japan

Cover: Foto ©Andreas Hilbeck / pixelio.de

More available books at **www.hansebooks.com**

A Tale Told by Documents

Cupid's Game With Hearts

Cupid's Game with Hearts

❦ ❦ ❦

A TALE AS TOLD BY DOCUMENTS

❦ ❦ ❦

ILLUSTRATED BY

STELLA ALYS WITTRAM

TWENTY-FIRST THOUSAND

DODGE PUBLISHING COMPANY
40-42 EAST 19th STREET, NEW YORK

Tuesday morning
March 24 — 1896.
Dearest Kora,
            I'm just home
from Chicago and must see
you at once. Can you meet
me at lunch tomorrow? I
can scarcely wait till
I see you.
            Yours in haste
                  Lydia.

P.S.
      Oh Kora! I must tell
you just a little or I think
I shall explode. I became
acquainted with a gentleman

in the cars, and you have no
idea how kind he was to me
in many little ways. He had
a letter of introduction to
papa, and when we were
nearing the city he gave
me his card and said he
would never forget me. His
name is Hector Arlington.
I think he is poor for it was
in his own hand writing.
But now comes the awful
bit. At the depot, who should
be waiting for me but —
Count Houski. He was quite
impudent to Mr. E. and
there would have been a
scene — but I must tell
you the rest tomorrow. I
never longed so much for

Dear Miss Partington

After the incident at the depot
this afternoon, I think it only justice
to myself to put an end to the
anomalous position which I have
been occupying.

I considered I was bestowing
upon you some honour when I
intimated, six months ago that I
should be much gratified by
giving you the title of Countess
And though I said I would gladly
allow you plenty of time to

reconsider, I feel that in justice
to myself that time has now
come to an end.

As you have not been at home
to me on the last two occasions
on which I did myself the pleasure
of calling ere you left for
Chicago, may I request that you
favor me with an interview at
Eleven o'clock on Wednesday. Mr
Partington has always treated me
like a gentleman, and has
often assured me that my suit
had his cordial approval.

Accept the assurance of my
devotion
                    Horeski

Monday evening

"PAPA CAME HOME ALL OUT OF TEMPER"

Tuesday - 8.30 P.M.

Dearest Kora.

I had your note
this morning by messenger.
So you can't come tomorrow
because the Count desires to
see you at 10 o'clock. Well
I have a letter from the
same gentleman, asking
me to meet him at 11!
Oh the scheme! Saying

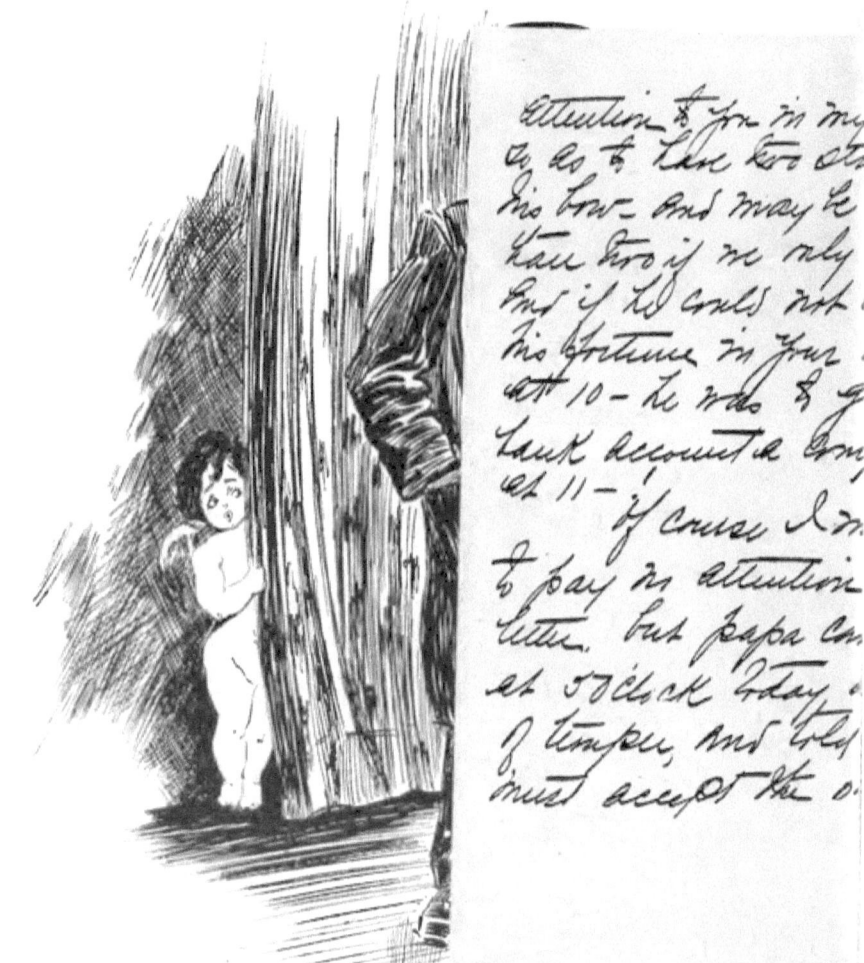

"PAPA CAME HOME ALL OUT OF TEMPER."

man within twenty four
hours. He is to call
tomorrow at eleven for his
yes or no. I can't see
why papa is so set upon
the match. Oh Karl —
as you love me, when he
makes his call on you
tomorrow, ask him to
spend the afternoon in
order to meet some friends
anything to let me gain
a little time.
Your distracted
Lydia.

RATHER HARD ON HORESKI.

A ROW ON BROADWAY IN WHICH THE COUNT FARED BADLY.

It was a dense crowd that surged in front of Partington, Selanders & Co.'s yesterday morning about ten o'clock. Everyone seemed bent on seeing the fight which was in full swing on the sidewalk. Owing to the limited stature of one of the combatants—a fat little man in a fur-lined overcoat, who gave as his name Count Horeski—nothing could be seen but the head and shoulders of a tall young fellow, who seemed to be holding and shaking something as a terrier might do a rat.

The police at last arrived on the scene and terrier and rat were taken to the station. There matters were satisfactorily arranged, and the Count emerged still much agitated and with neck-gear rather out of order. "I have really no complaint to make," said Count Horeski. "The young man accosted me rather familiarly, so as to attract attention; I have, however, really no complaint to make."

The young man, who refused to give his name, when seen on his homeward way, seemed to view the matter in a somewhat different light, as he admitted that it was his earnest desire to shake a little impertinence out of the Count so as to make him more fit for ladies' society.

On investigation, however, it seems that matters were not so smooth as the answer of the Count would imply. The Count has made himself famous lately by his connection with the Marsden mining scheme and has been doing his very best to develop another plot just as interesting to the general public. So,

Dear Lydia,
        Our mutual
admirer, the Count, did
not keep his appoint-
ment yesterday, but
appeared this forenoon
instead.

He made profuse
apologies, stating he had
had a most serious
street accident the
nature of which he did
not divulge.

Asked if I had seen

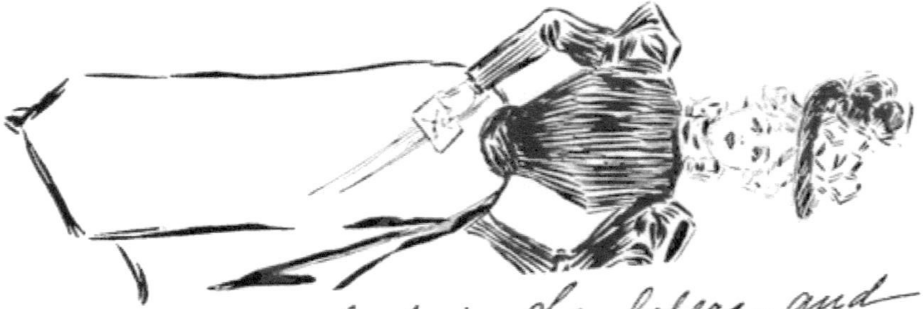

changing of my present happy condition

It impatients me the adventure of an attendance with the great family of Frank, which can there its decision from Adam — into a poor innocent timber.

There be nice to go, but asked if I would not reconsider." "Count Frankie" said I, "is my statement true, we will have no more to fear of your being an [illegible]

And so that is me, and I have not — wing my fate yet. — Fina

From the *Evening Sun*

FAILURE OF A LARGE DRY GOODS CONCERN.

The failure is reported of the well-known dry goods firm of Partington, Selanders & Co. Various causes are assigned, the most probable being the large amount of cash withdrawn by Solomon Selanders when he retired from the firm a year ago. Much sympathy is felt for the sole remaining partner, who must have been bearing a heavy burden in the administration and financeering of his colossal business. 13c.

From Friday's *Times*

SAD SEQUEL TO THURSDAY'S MELEE ON BROADWAY.

William W. Corderwell, the millionaire real estate owner and railroad king, died very suddenly last night. His end was undoubtedly hastened by learning what had been, in consideration of his critical state of health, carefully kept from him. The news that his favorite nephew had laid hands on Count Horeski, threw the deceased gentleman into such a state of agitation that he burst a blood-vessel. Death resulted within an hour thereafter.   15c.

The Mayfield
Brooklyn, March 30th, 1896.

My Dear Miss Partington,

I know that you will not think me forward in writing to you to express my deepest sympathy. The pleasant time we had on board the cars has imbued me with some feeling of partnership in this catastrophe. I am glad of such feeling, and more glad still that the event opens up to me even a possibility of greater nearness to your dear self. Since we said, Goodbye, your image has been before me day and night. I never thought myself romantic, but, if the carrying about with me ever since a tiny glove, be romance, I plead guilty, as I do of the theft. I was hopeless of ever possessing anything more of yours, and sorely

needed something to comfort me.

It was not for one as poor as I to intrude further acquaintance upon you, but the events of the last few days make it possible, to my great joy — Through the death of an Uncle, I shall have enough to promise you, with all safety, a Home, if you will accept it. I shall only promise, in the meantime, a plain Home; but, if you take me along with it, I venture to say it will be a happy one.

This dear little glove is empty, and wants a hand to fill it. It is solitary, and wants a mate. May I one to you, and plead face to face?

Devotedly yours.

Hector Arlington

A brief answer

TELEGRAM

POSTAL TELEGRAPH-CABLE COMPANY.

This Company transmits and delivers messages subject to the terms and conditions printed on the back of this blank.

JOHN O. STEVENS, Secretary.   ALBERT B. CHANDLER, President and General Manager.

3r. Wizfet 10 am Mar 31/96

New York 9 am Mar 31/9

Received at Brooklyn

(WHERE ANY REPLY SHOULD BE SENT.)

Hector Arlington
Brooklyn

Come

Lydia Partington

Midnight. Mar 31- 1896.

Dearest Kora.

I'm so happy now I simply can't keep from writing you a few lines. The Trouble Cloud is gone and that awful failure cloud is gone and I'm looking up at the starlit sky and feeling the warm sunshine all through me although the clock says it's midnight.

He has just left — Hector my own darling Hector I can say that now for we are engaged! And he played such a joke on me. The

Oh Kora! I'm so happy I've
danced three times round
the room, and everything is
in a whirl of joy. But
Hector and I are not
going to be selfish with our
money, — we mean to do
lots of good. And now
goodnight Kora my
Brides-maid-to-be.
         Your happy
              Sydia.

From the society page of the *Herald*

The engagement is announced of Hector Arlington, only son of the late Hezekiah Arlington, and Miss Lydia Partington, only daughter of Joseph Partington of this city. The wedding will take place early in June. 23e.

MARSHALL, LITTLEFIELD & SIMKINS

ATTORNEYS AT LAW

SAN FRANCISCO

June 2nd, 1896.

Hector Arlington, Esq.,

    CITY.

Dear Sir:

    We regret to inform you that a Will of later date to that in which you were interested, has been offered for probate, bequeathing all the Real and Personal Property of your deceased uncle to his cousin, Amanda Peterson.

    We shall be glad to have a call from you at your earliest convenience.

        Your obedient servants,

        Marshall, Littlefield & Simkins.

Dictated.

June 15th 1896.

Dearest,

I have sad news for you.
I have just returned from seeing my
lawyers about a letter they sent me,
stating that there is a later will of my
Uncle's, in which he has bequeathed everything to some Cousin, of whom I rarely
heard him speak.

I feel too downcast to call. Our
Marriage is now impossible; my helping
your Father also out of the question
I can only with a very, very sad
heart release you from all promises
and say a hopeless Goodbye to you.
I cannot write more, with all that
beautiful castle in which you were
to dwell, lying in ruins around me

Hector

My dear Heston

I have a good
mind to scold you. Do
you think that my love
for you depends on
your wealth? I will
not even sympathize
with you, for you have
no real need in this
world except some one
to stand by you when
you are down.

If a little money
left me by my mother—

will be of any use in furnishing our little house and you are willing to keep me in it, I dont see why any second will need interfere with our own sweet first will which is to respond I will on a very interesting occasion. As to papa — his creditors have offered to lend him money — give him time — do anything, in fact, to

From the *New York Times*

The wedding of Miss Lydia Partington and Hector Arlington took place last Wednesday at the residence of the bride's father.